Activity Book

God's Big Christmas Plan

Written by: Wendy van Leeuwen
Designed by: Kevin Spear

Warner
Press Kids™
educate • nurture • inspire
www.warnerpress.org

Christmas Joy

Christmas is a special time. We celebrate Jesus' birth because He came to save us from our sins. (Related scriptures: Isaiah 7:14, Matthew 1:23)

Can you find all of the Christmas words hidden in this puzzle?

A	T	R	E	S	O	M	R	N	I	T
O	J	S	T	A	B	L	E	S	N	V
X	I	A	T	W	J	C	E	R	N	J
M	L	V	U	T	M	J	V	N	E	S
A	Y	I	R	Q	J	O	S	E	P	H
G	L	O	R	Y	N	Y	V	G	J	E
I	O	R	M	E	Q	A	S	D	F	P
P	I	Y	T	N	B	W	C	A	X	H
E	J	E	S	U	S	M	S	N	F	E
P	L	K	T	J	M	A	N	G	E	R
O	P	E	A	C	E	R	H	E	G	D
U	I	Y	R	T	R	Y	E	L	W	S

ANGEL	JOSEPH	MARY	SHEPHERDS
GLORY	JOY	PEACE	STABLE
INN	MAGI	SAVIOR	STAR
JESUS	MANGER		

Answer on page 43

The Beginning

The Christmas story began long before Jesus was born in Bethlehem. Jesus was already with God when the world was created. Perhaps they talked about how many legs an octopus should have, or how to make maple keys twirl, or which colors to paint the butterflies (Genesis 1, John 1:1-3).

Color by number to decorate your own butterfly.

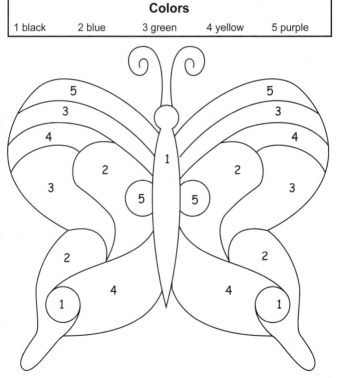

Colors				
1 black	2 blue	3 green	4 yellow	5 purple

Creation

God created the world in six days. Everything He created was good and perfect (Genesis 1, 2).

What did God make on each day? Look in your Bible at Genesis 1 to find the answers for this puzzle. The letters in each column fit into the squares directly below them, but not usually in the same order. There are black squares at the beginning and end of each word. Hint: cross off each letter in pencil as you use it.

	L	I	S	N	K	M	O	A	S	B	P	T	O	R	T	E
	F	A	A	N	Y	M	A	N	N	G	P	R	A	N	L	S
		S	D	A	I	Y	E	O	S		S	E	D	P	S	
		U	H		S		L	I			H	L	A	S		
		N	D								I	T				
			S													

Day 1													
Day 2													
Day 3													
Day 4													
Day 5													
Day 6													

4

Answer on page 43

Rebellion

Adam and Eve listened to the devil's lies and ate some fruit from the tree that God had placed off-limits. This disobedience broke their friendship with God.

Read Genesis 3:1-9 and fill in the blanks in the paragraph then fit the answers into the grid.

The _ _ _ _ _ _ _ (1) was more crafty than any of the wild animals God had made.

God told Adam and Eve, "Do not eat the _ _ _ _ _ (2) from the tree in the middle of the _ _ _ _ _ _ (3), or you will die." But the serpent said, "You will be like God, knowing _ _ _ _ (4) and _ _ _ _ (5)." The woman took some fruit and gave some to her husband, and they _ _ _ (6) it. Then their eyes were opened, and they were ashamed, so they hid among the _ _ _ _ _ (7). But God called to them, "_ _ _ _ _ (8) are you?"

1.
2.
3.
&
4.
5.
6.
7.
8.

Read the highlighted area from top to bottom. What came into the world when Adam and Eve chose to disobey God?

_____ & _____

Answer on page 43

God's Promise

Even before He banished Adam and Eve from the garden, God was planning for the first Christmas. He would send someone to pay the price for sin and disobedience. He would make it possible for us to be forgiven and to have a friendship with God again (Genesis 3:15, John 3:16).

Who did God send? Decode the message by substituting each letter with the letter that comes two places after it in the alphabet. For example, A becomes C, M becomes O, Z goes back around to the beginning to become B.

A B C D E F G H I J K L M N O P Q R S T U V W X Y Z

DMP   EMB   QM   JMTCB   RFC   UMPJB   FC

_____

EYTC   FGQ   MLC   YLB   MLJW   QML   RFYR

_____

UFMCTCP   ZCJGCTCQ   GL   FGK   UGJJ

_____

LCTCP   BGC   ZSR   FYTC   CRCPLYJ   JGDC

_____

Answer on page 43

Christmas Prophecy

God used prophets, priests and kings during Old Testament times to prepare His people for the coming of the Messiah, Jesus (Isaiah 9, 53).

The Prophet Isaiah used many names and descriptions for Jesus. See if you can find them in this word search.

L	Q	Y	P	E	R	I	U	K	K	T	I
A	S	E	R	V	A	N	T	W	I	B	S
M	T	G	I	E	P	E	A	J	N	P	O
B	H	J	N	R	K	B	C	Z	G	C	V
J	S	R	C	L	I	G	H	T	R	O	M
L	A	F	E	A	D	K	O	Q	K	U	D
H	V	R	A	S	S	D	S	I	B	N	C
M	I	G	H	T	Y	E	E	A	X	S	R
C	O	E	N	I	H	F	N	M	W	E	V
D	R	W	O	N	D	E	R	F	U	L	P
T	M	B	E	G	U	T	R	L	X	O	Z
K	F	S	R	E	D	E	E	M	E	R	B

CHOSEN	LIGHT	COUNSELOR	MIGHTY
EVERLASTING	PRINCE	FATHER	REDEEMER
GOD	SAVIOR	KING	SERVANT
LAMB	WONDERFUL		

Answer on page 43

We Have Seen God's Glory

A prophecy is a statement about something God will do in the future. There are many prophecies about Jesus in the Old Testament.

Find the prophecy from Isaiah 9:6 hidden in this letter maze. Write it on the lines below.

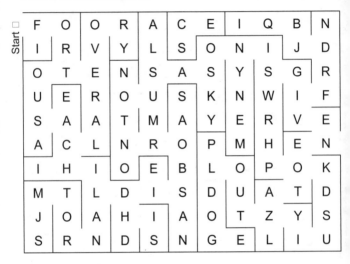

_____

_____

Answer on page 43

A Special Baby

An angel appeared to Mary to tell her she would have a very special baby. His name would be Jesus, and He would be God's own Son (Luke 1:26-38).

Using pencils, crayons or markers, color by number to reveal the hidden picture.

Colors			
1 white	2 orange	3 yellow	4 light brown
5 black	6 light blue	7 blue	8 dark blue

Give Him the Name Jesus

How surprised Mary must have been to hear the angel's amazing news! She had been chosen to be the mother of God's Son, Jesus (Luke 1:31, 32).

Starting at the bold **H** in the corner, enter it on the first space below, then follow the arrow to find out which letter comes next. Continue writing down each letter and following the arrows until you've discovered the entire message.

H→	E↓	N→	D→	W→	I↓
O↓	W↓	A↑	T←	M←	L↓
L↓	I←	E→	A↑	B↓	L←
L↓	P↑	R↑	K↑	E↓	C↑
B→	E→	G↑	F↓	C→	A↓
N↓	O←	H↓	T←	B←	L↓
O↓	S↑	E←	D↑	E←	L←
F↓	E→	M↓	L↓	S↑	Q←
T→	H↑	O↓	W↓	I→	G↓
P←	J↓	S→	T→	H↑	H.

__ ____ __

_____ ___ ____

__ _____ ____ ___

___ __ ___

____ ____ ____.

Answer on page 44

John the Baptist

Mary's relative Elizabeth also had a baby. When he grew up he was called John the Baptist. He taught people to make their hearts ready for Jesus (Luke 1:11-17).

Help Mary choose which path she should follow to get to Elizabeth's home.

Answer on page 44

Zechariah

When John the Baptist was born, his father Zechariah praised God and prophesied about the coming of Jesus (Luke 1:67-79).

Use the chart to match the letters with the numbers and decode some of Zechariah's words about Jesus.

$\overline{20}$ $\overline{8}$ $\overline{5}$ $\overline{18}$ $\overline{9}$ $\overline{19}$ $\overline{9}$ $\overline{14}$ $\overline{7}$

$\overline{19}$ $\overline{21}$ $\overline{14}$ $\overline{23}$ $\overline{9}$ $\overline{12}$ $\overline{12}$

$\overline{3}$ $\overline{15}$ $\overline{13}$ $\overline{5}$ $\overline{20}$ $\overline{15}$

$\overline{21}$ $\overline{19}$ $\overline{6}$ $\overline{18}$ $\overline{15}$ $\overline{13}$

$\overline{8}$ $\overline{5}$ $\overline{1}$ $\overline{22}$ $\overline{5}$ $\overline{14}$ $\overline{20}$ $\overline{15}$

$\overline{19}$ $\overline{8}$ $\overline{9}$ $\overline{14}$ $\overline{5}$ $\overline{15}$ $\overline{14}$

$\overline{20}$ $\overline{8}$ $\overline{15}$ $\overline{19}$ $\overline{5}$

$\overline{12}$ $\overline{9}$ $\overline{22}$ $\overline{9}$ $\overline{14}$ $\overline{7}$ $\overline{9}$ $\overline{14}$

$\overline{4}$ $\overline{1}$ $\overline{18}$ $\overline{11}$ $\overline{14}$ $\overline{5}$ $\overline{19}$ $\overline{19}$.

A	B	C	D	E	F	G	H	I	J	K	L	M
1	2	3	4	5	6	7	8	9	10	11	12	13
N	O	P	Q	R	S	T	U	V	W	X	Y	Z
14	15	16	17	18	19	20	21	22	23	24	25	26

   Answer on page 44

Joseph

God chose a man named Joseph to be Jesus' earthly father. He was a godly man and a member of King David's family. Joseph made his living as a carpenter (Matthew 1:18-25).

Fit the carpentry words into the crossword grid. Hint: count the number of letters to help you decide where they should go.

carving	nails	sander
file	plane	saw
hammer	rasp	wood

Immanuel

An angel appeared to Joseph in a dream and told him that Mary was going to have a very special baby—God's own son. He would be called Immanuel (Matthew 1:23, Isaiah 7:14).

Starting at the outside end of the spiral, write every third letter (3, 6, 9…) on the lines below to find out what the name Immanuel means.

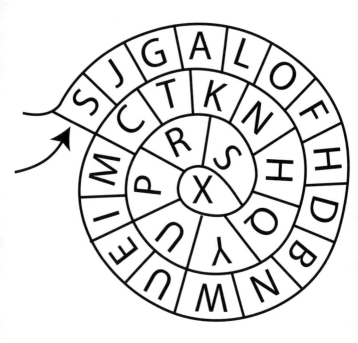

__ __ __ __   __ __ __ __ __   __ __

Answer on page 44

Celebrate!

Why do we celebrate at Christmas time? Because God loves us so much that He sent His son Jesus to be born and to die for us (Related scriptures: John 3:16, Matthew 1:21).

Cross out the letters K, Q, X and D. The left over letters spell out the angel's words to Joseph, and tell why Jesus was born. Write them on the lines below.

Q	Y	O	U	X	K	A	R	E	D	X	T	O	Q	K	D
G	I	V	E	D	K	Q	H	I	M	Q	K	D	T	H	E
Q	K	N	A	M	E	X	K	Q	J	E	S	U	S	K	Q
K	D	Q	B	E	C	A	U	S	E	X	K	X	H	E	X
W	I	L	L	D	K	Q	S	A	V	E	Q	H	I	S	K
D	K	X	K	P	E	O	P	L	E	X	K	D	K	Q	D
Q	F	R	O	M	Q	K	Q	T	H	E	I	R	K	X	Q
X	K	D	S	I	N	S	D	K	Q	D	K	Q	X	K	Q

_____

_____

_____

Answer on page 44

Traveling to Bethlehem

Joseph and Mary went to Bethlehem to register with the government, because the ruler of Rome wanted to know how many people lived in his empire. It was a long, difficult journey, especially for Mary, whose baby was almost ready to be born. Perhaps she rode on a donkey while Joseph walked in front (Luke 2:1-3).

Today we have many ways to travel from one place to another. Can you unscramble the words to spell out different types of transportation?

A T R N I   _____

T B A O   _____

E T F E   _____

A R C   _____

S U B   _____

L N E P I R A A   _____

E K B I   _____

Answer on page 45

No Room in the Inn

When Mary and Joseph arrived in Bethlehem, the only place they could find to rest was in a stable behind an inn. When Jesus was born, His parents wrapped Him in strips of cloth and laid Him in a manger for a bed (Luke 2).

Shade in the numbered squares according to the key.

Key						
1=■	2=◣	3=◤	4=◹	5=◺	6=◧	7=◨

		2	3															
		2	3							5	2							
		1	1			3	4			4	3							
2	2	1	1	1	1	3	3		2	5					3	4		
5	5	1	1	1	1	4	4								2	5		
		1	1							2	3							
		1	1				2	1	1	1	1	3						
		5	4		2	1	1	1	4	5	1	1	1	3				
		5	4	2	1	1	1	4			5	1	1	1	3			
			2	1	1	1	4					5	1	1	1	3		
3			1										5	1	1			
1	3		1											1	1			
1	1	3	1											1	1			
6	7		1										5	1				
6	7		1		2	6				7	3			1				
1	1		1		1	6				7	1			1				
1	1		1	2	1	3				2	1	3		1				
			1	1	1		5	1	1	4	1	1	3	1				
			1	2	1	1	1		2		3	1	1	1	3	1		

Born in a Stable

A stable is an animal shed. It was a humble place for the Son of God to be born. Perhaps some animals watched Him as He slept in their feedbox (Philippians 2:6-11).

Can you match these animal mothers with their babies?

Mare	Cub
Cow	Chick
Bear	Lamb
Swan	Foal
Kangaroo	Cygnet
Sheep	Calf
Cat	Gosling
Fish	Puppy
Goose	Kitten
Dog	Joey
Hen	Fingerling

Answer on page 45

Christmas is Spelled L-O-V-E

Jesus Christ, eternal God and creator of heaven and earth, was born as a helpless human baby in Bethlehem. This is the most important event in all history. Without the first Christmas we could never be saved from our sins (John 1:14, Luke 2, Matthew 1, 2).

Fill in the missing letters in these Christmas words, and then enter them into the numbered spaces.

GI _ TS   A _ GELS   SHEP _ ER _ S
   13   7   9   3

LO _ E   S _ ABL _   _ IS _ MEN
   16   8   22   11   21

MAR _   JE _ U _   IMM _ N _ EL
    5   17 19   4   23

ST _ R   J _ SEPH   _ E _ HLEH _ M
   15   2   20 1   10

HERO _   MA _ GE _   MESS _ AH
      14   12   18   6

$\overline{1}\ \overline{2}\ \overline{3}\ \overline{4}\ \overline{5}$ $\overline{6}\ \overline{7}$ $\overline{8}\ \overline{9}\ \overline{10}$ $\overline{1}\ \overline{2}\ \overline{11}\ \overline{12}$

$\overline{2}\ \overline{13}$ $\overline{14}\ \overline{15}\ \overline{16}\ \overline{6}\ \overline{3}$ $\overline{4}$

$\overline{17}\ \overline{15}\ \overline{16}\ \overline{6}\ \overline{2}\ \overline{18}$ $\overline{9}\ \overline{4}\ \overline{19}$ $\overline{20}\ \overline{21}\ \overline{22}\ \overline{7}$

$\overline{20}\ \overline{2}\ \overline{18}\ \overline{12}$ $\overline{8}\ \overline{2}$ $\overline{5}\ \overline{2}\ \overline{23}$.

Shepherds Hear the News

Some shepherds watching their sheep in the fields near Bethlehem were the first to hear the good news. "Today in the town of David a Savior has been born to you; he is Christ the Lord" (Luke 2:11).

Which two sheep are exactly the same? Look carefully!

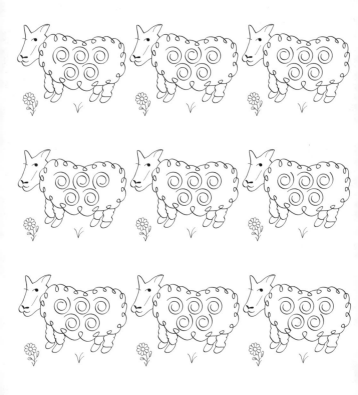

Answer on page 45

Peace on Earth

The frightened shepherds listened in amazement as a choir of angels filled the night sky with songs of praise to God. Then they ran to Bethlehem to see baby Jesus themselves (Luke 2).

Fit the letter blocks into the spaces to spell out the angels' song. Some letters have been filled in for you.

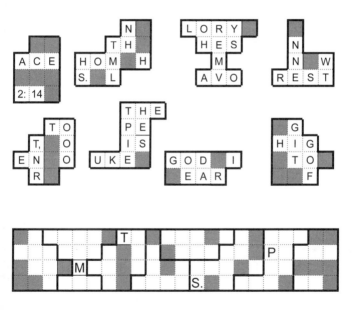

Answer on page 45

21

A Special Star

A wonderful new star appeared in the sky when Jesus was born. Astrologers from a distant country, called Magi, saw the star and knew it meant a new king had been born in Judea (Matthew 2:2).

Draw a line between the points listed to draw a surprise picture. The first one is done for you.

D 2□D 10   D 2□L 6   L 6□D 10   I 2□A 6   A 6□I 10   I 10□I 2

Answer on page 45

Following a Star

The Magi followed the star from their home in the East to Jerusalem. They visited King Herod and asked him about the new King of the Jews (Matthew 2).

All of the answers to these clues end with the word KING.

1. Doing a job.   __ __ __ K I N G

2. Preparing a cake in an oven.   __ __ K I N G

3. Pretending.   __ __ K I N G

4. Seeing something.   __ __ __ K I N G

5. Telling a funny story.   __ __ K I N G

6. Preparing food on the stove.   __ __ __ K I N G

7. Pedaling a two-wheeler.   __ __ K I N G

8. Using words to communicate.   __ __ __ K I N G

9. Opening and closing your eyes quickly.   __ __ __ __ K I N G

10. Traveling to another place on foot.   __ __ __ K I N G

Answer on page 46

The Gifts of the Magi

The Magi traveled to Bethlehem to worship Jesus. They brought gold, frankincense and myrrh—the first Christmas presents (Matthew 2:9-12).

Have fun decorating these Christmas gifts with markers or crayons. Don't forget ribbons and bows!

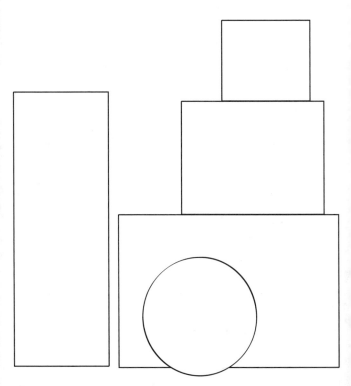

Star of Royal Beauty

In the Old Testament book of Numbers the prophet Balaam talked about the coming of Jesus. "A star will come out of Jacob; a scepter will rise out of Israel" (Numbers 24:17). And in the last book of the Bible, Revelation, Jesus describes Himself as the bright Morning Star (Revelation 22:16).

Make your own Star Ornament

1. Draw a triangle on card stock or cereal box cardboard. All three sides of the triangle must be the same length. Four inches (10 cm) per side is a good size, but you can make it bigger if you like.

2. Cut the triangle out with scissors. Ask a grown up to help if it is difficult to cut.

3. Trace around the triangle to make another one exactly the same, and cut it out.

4. Glue one triangle on top of the other. Turn it so that the points are equal all around.

5. Decorate using markers, glitter, paint, or sequins and let it dry.

6. Using a hole punch, make a hole in one of the points. Cut a piece of ribbon or yarn about six inches (15 cm) long and tie it through the hole.

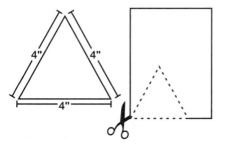

And He Will Be Called...

When Jesus was eight days old His parents gave Jesus His name in a special ceremony. Hundreds of years before Jesus was born, the prophet Isaiah predicted His birth and used some other special names for Jesus (Isaiah 9, 53).

Find these other names for Jesus in the chart. You will need to follow the words around corners. The first one is done for you.

MAN OF SORROWS

RIGHTEOUS SERVANT

WONDERFUL COUNSELOR

MIGHTY GOD

EVERLASTING FATHER

PRINCE OF PEACE

LIGHT

M	P	R	I	F	P	T	H	G	I
A	N	O	N	O	E	A	C	E	L
H	E	F	C	E	G	O	R	E	S
T	R	S	H	T	Y	D	V	R	S
A	R	O	G	F	U	L	A	O	U
F	R	M	I	R	E	C	N	L	O
G	O	W	S	E	V	O	T	E	E
N	W	O	N	D	E	U	N	S	T
I	T	S	A	L	R	R	I	G	H

Answer on page 46

Simeon

When **JESUS**' parents brought Him to the **TEMPLE** to dedicate Him to **GOD**, an old man named **SIMEON** took Jesus in his arms and praised God, saying:

"Sovereign **LORD**, as you have **PROMISED**, you now dismiss your **SERVANT** in **PEACE**. For my eyes have seen your **SALVATION**, which you have prepared in the sight of all **PEOPLE**, a **LIGHT** for revelation to the **GENTILES** and for **GLORY** to your people **ISRAEL**" (Luke 2:29-32).

Fit the words in CAPITAL letters above into the puzzle grid. Hint: count the number of letters. All spaces needing a letter **S** have been filled in to get you started.

Answer on page 46

Escape to Egypt

When Herod, King of Judea, heard that God's Son had been born in Bethlehem he became very worried. He did not want to give up his throne to a new king. God sent an angel to warn Joseph that Herod would try to kill Jesus. Joseph, Mary and Jesus quickly escaped to the country of Egypt (Matthew 2:2-18).

Find your way through the maze from Bethlehem to Egypt.

Bethlehem▼

Egypt▲

Answer on page 46

Jesus' Life

"[Jesus] grew and became strong; he was filled with wisdom, and the grace of God was upon him" (Luke 2:40).

Here is a game for you to play with 2 to 4 players. You will need something small to mark your place. Take turns tossing a coin. **Heads** moves forward 3 spaces, **tails** moves back one.

Start	An angel appears to Mary	Jesus is born in Bethlehem	* Jump forward 2 spaces	Shepherds hear the news	Magi come to worship	
					Escape to Egypt	
	Jesus is tempted by Satan	John baptizes Jesus	* Miss a turn	Jesus visits the temple	Herod kills Bethlehem's baby boys	
	Beginning of Jesus' ministry					
	Jesus chooses the Disciples	Sermon on the Mount	Jesus performs miracles	* Go back 2 spaces	Jesus teaches in parables	
					Jesus is transfigured	
	Jesus is crucified on the cross	* Take an extra turn	Lord's Supper	Jesus rides into Jerusalem	Children invited to meet Jesus	
	Jesus is raised to life					
	Jesus gives The Great Commission	Jesus ascends to heaven	* Go back 1 space	The Holy Spirit comes	The Church grows	Finish

Jesus Grows Up

When Jesus was twelve years old, He went missing while on a family trip to the city of Jerusalem. His parents searched for three days before they found Jesus in the temple, talking to the religious teachers (Luke 2:41-50).

Can you find your way through the maze?
Take your time, it's tricky!

Answer on page 46

John the Baptist

John was a prophet, sent to prepare the way for Jesus and His ministry. When he baptized Jesus in the Jordan River, the Holy Spirit came down like a dove and God spoke from heaven (Luke 3; John 1:29).

Cross out all the letters that appear four times in the grid. Then write the leftover letters on the lines, in order, to finish a verse about Jesus.

C	L	E	J	A	K	H	P
Q	X	U	M	X	Z	T	B
E	K	F	T	G	V	Q	Z
V	F	C	Y	Y	H	O	U
D	U	H	S	Z	P	K	J
Y	I	P	F	X	N	Y	Q
P	C	V	E	S	E	J	W
T	X	O	Z	K	T	V	R
L	J	C	Q	H	U	D	F

"Look! The __ __ __ __ of __ __ __,

who takes away the __ __ __ __ of the

__ __ __ __ __."

Answer on page 46

Jesus Begins His Ministry

Jesus chose twelve men to be His disciples. They helped Jesus in His work, witnessed His miracles and learned about the kingdom of God. We can be disciples of Jesus today by reading His words in the Bible and believing in Him (Matthew 10:2-4).

Fit the names of the twelve disciples into the framework. One letter has been placed in the puzzle to get you started.

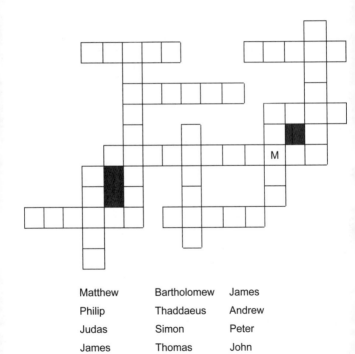

Matthew	Bartholomew	James
Philip	Thaddaeus	Andrew
Judas	Simon	Peter
James	Thomas	John

Answer on page 47

Good Friday

As Jesus hung dying on the cross, people mocked Him. "If you really are the Son of God, save yourself. Come down from the cross!" Jesus could have come down but He obeyed God's plan. His suffering and death were the only way to pay for the sins of the world (Matthew 27:40-43, 2 Corinthians 5:21).

What was Jesus' answer to those who insulted Him? Solve the riddles and enter the letters from the answers into the matching spaces in the phrase below.

A green amphibian.

$\overline{10}$ $\overline{6}$ $\overline{13}$ $\overline{14}$

Narrow strip of water around a castle.

$\overline{17}$ $\overline{13}$ $\overline{7}$ $\overline{11}$

To jump headfirst into water.

$\overline{9}$ $\overline{15}$ $\overline{16}$ $\overline{2}$

The opposite of PULL.

$\overline{5}$ $\overline{4}$ $\overline{3}$ $\overline{12}$

Popular Christmas hymn: "_ _ _ to the World".

$\overline{1}$ $\overline{13}$ $\overline{8}$

$\overline{1}$ $\overline{2}$ $\overline{3}$ $\overline{4}$ $\overline{3}$ $\overline{5}$ $\overline{6}$ $\overline{7}$ $\overline{8}$ $\overline{2}$ $\overline{9}$

$\overline{10}$ $\overline{7}$ $\overline{11}$ $\overline{12}$ $\overline{2}$ $\overline{6}$ $\overline{10}$ $\overline{13}$ $\overline{6}$ $\overline{14}$ $\overline{15}$ $\overline{16}$ $\overline{2}$

$\overline{11}$ $\overline{12}$ $\overline{2}$ $\overline{17}$.

Answer on page 47

Light in the Darkness

"The light shines in the darkness, but the darkness has not understood it" (John 1:5). Jesus came to rescue us from the darkness of sin and bring us into the warm light of God's love.

Draw a line to connect a group of letters from column **A** with a group from column **B** to make the names of "light" things.

A	**B**
FLASH	RISE
LIGHT	FLY
RAIN	NING
SUN	LIGHT
CAN	FIRE
LAN	BULB
LIGHT	LIGHT
CAMP	SHINE
FIRE	TERN
STAR	BOW
SUN	DLE

Answer on page 47

The King of Zion

"See, your king comes to you, righteous and having salvation, gentle and riding on a donkey, on a colt, the foal of a donkey. He will proclaim peace to the nations" (Zechariah 9:9-10).

Jesus did not come to earth wearing a crown and commanding an army. He came as a helpless infant. He taught us how to love our neighbors and to walk humbly with God.

Connect the dots and color.

God is Love

Do you know how much God loves you?

Use the chart to match the letters with the numbers and decode a verse about His love (1John 4).

$\overline{20}\ \overline{8}\ \overline{9}\ \overline{19}$ $\overline{9}\ \overline{19}$ $\overline{8}\ \overline{15}\ \overline{23}$

$\overline{7}\ \overline{15}\ \overline{4}$ $\overline{19}\ \overline{8}\ \overline{15}\ \overline{23}\ \overline{5}\ \overline{4}$ $\overline{8}\ \overline{9}\ \overline{19}$

$\overline{12}\ \overline{15}\ \overline{22}\ \overline{5}$ $\overline{1}\ \overline{13}\ \overline{15}\ \overline{14}\ \overline{7}$

$\overline{21}\ \overline{19}:$ $\overline{8}\ \overline{5}$ $\overline{19}\ \overline{5}\ \overline{14}\ \overline{20}$ $\overline{8}\ \overline{9}\ \overline{19}$

$\overline{15}\ \overline{14}\ \overline{5}$ $\overline{1}\ \overline{14}\ \overline{4}$ $\overline{15}\ \overline{14}\ \overline{12}\ \overline{25}$

$\overline{19}\ \overline{15}\ \overline{14}$ $\overline{9}\ \overline{14}\ \overline{20}\ \overline{15}$ $\overline{20}\ \overline{8}\ \overline{5}$

$\overline{23}\ \overline{15}\ \overline{18}\ \overline{12}\ \overline{4}.$

A	B	C	D	E	F	G	H	I	J	K	L	M
1	2	3	4	5	6	7	8	9	10	11	12	13
N	O	P	Q	R	S	T	U	V	W	X	Y	Z
14	15	16	17	18	19	20	21	22	23	24	25	26

Answer on page 47

Eden to Easter

Jesus is the answer to the promise God made in the Garden of Eden. When He rose from the dead on Easter morning, He won the victory over sin and death for us (1 John 3:1, John 12:27, John 3:16).

α	β	χ	δ	ε	φ	γ	η	ι	φ	κ	λ	μ	ν	o	π	θ	ρ	σ	τ	υ	φ	ω	ξ	ψ	ζ
a	b	c	d	e	f	g	h	i	j	k	l	m	n	o	p	q	r	s	t	u	v	w	x	y	z

Use the alphabet chart to translate the words in the cross.

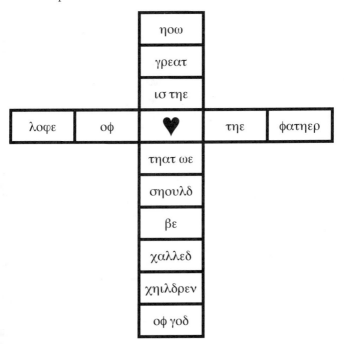

ηοω

γρεατ

ισ τηε

λοφε   οφ   ♥   τηε   φατηερ

τηατ ωε

σηουλδ

βε

χαλλεδ

χηιλδρεν

οφ γοδ

Answer on page 47

Power over Death

Jesus died but after three days God brought Him back to life. An angel came and rolled the large stone away from His tomb. The angel was bright like lightning and the women who came to the tomb to cry for Jesus were terrified when they saw him (Matthew 28:1-10).

What did the angel say? Use the chart below to find out. The number on the left comes first in each pair. For example, X is 5/4.

	1	2	3	4	5
1	A	B	C	D	E
2	F	G	H	I	J
3	K	L	M	N	O
4	P	Q	R	S	T
5	U	V	W	X	Y

$\overline{1/4}$ $\overline{3/5}$　$\overline{3/4}$ $\overline{3/5}$ $\overline{4/5}$　$\overline{1/2}$ $\overline{1/5}$

$\overline{1/1}$ $\overline{2/1}$ $\overline{4/3}$ $\overline{1/1}$ $\overline{2/4}$ $\overline{1/4}$　$\overline{2/3}$ $\overline{1/5}$　$\overline{2/4}$ $\overline{4/4}$

$\overline{3/4}$ $\overline{3/5}$ $\overline{4/5}$　$\overline{2/3}$ $\overline{1/5}$ $\overline{4/3}$ $\overline{1/5}$　$\overline{2/3}$ $\overline{1/5}$

$\overline{2/3}$ $\overline{1/1}$ $\overline{4/4}$　$\overline{4/3}$ $\overline{2/4}$ $\overline{4/4}$ $\overline{1/5}$ $\overline{3/4}$

Answer on page 47

Back to Heaven

Jesus went back to heaven to sit on His throne at the right hand of God. He sent the Holy Spirit to live in our hearts so we can love and obey God (Matthew 28:16-20).

What instruction did Jesus give to us before He went to heaven? Using the ruler below, follow the arrows to decode the answer.

<u>G</u> __   __ __ __   __ __ __ __

__ __ __ __ __ __ __ __ __.

Starting at **G** on the ruler (already filled in), jump forward (→) **8** places on the ruler. Enter the letter you land on in the next blank. Then, jump ←**14** and do the same thing.

- →13,
- ←10
- →9
- ←12
- →10
- ←6
- ←1
- →5

- →10
- ←16
- →6
- →7
- ←4
- ←7
- →14

Answer on page 48

Forgiveness

Christmas happened because God loves us so much. He sent His own son Jesus to pay for our sins so we can have a relationship with Him (John 3:16).

Fit the pieces into the puzzle grid to find out how each one of us can receive forgiveness for our sins and eternal life in heaven with God. Some letters have been filled in.

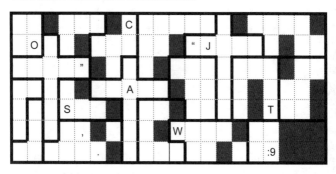

Answer on page 48

Christmas Traditions

Many families have Christmas traditions—a Christmas tree, advent candles, carol singing, exchanging gifts. It's fun to spend time together with the special people God has put in our lives.

Use crayons or colored pencils to complete this coloring grid.

Colors					
R=Red	B=Blue	G=Green	Y=Yellow	P=Purple	X=Brown

					Y					
				Y	Y	Y				
					Y					
					G					
				G	G	G				
			G	G	R	G	G			
		G	G	G	G	G	G	G		
				G	G	G				
			G	G	G	G	G			
		G	G	Y	G	G	G	G		
	G	G	G	G	G	R	G	G	G	
G	G	G	G	G	G	G	G	G	G	G
		G	R	G	G	G	G	G		
	G	G	G	G	G	G	Y	G	G	
G	G	G	G	G	G	G	G	G	G	G
G	Y	G	G	G	R	G	G	G	Y	G
G	G	G	G	G	G	G	G	G	G	G
				X	X	X				
P		B	R	B	B	X	P	Y	P	
Y		R	R	R	R		P	Y	P	
P		B	R	B	B		P	Y	P	

Christmas Word Builder

"The Lord God will give [Jesus] the throne of his father David, and he will reign over the house of Jacob forever; his kingdom will never end" (Luke 1:32-33).

Each symbol in the chart stands for the group of letters above it. Use the chart to fill in the empty spaces and build some Christmas words. The first one is done for you.

CHR	PHE	HEM	IM	IST	ITY	SHE
☺	♣	■	*	◉	╬	@

BET	MAN	EN	STA	HLE	GHT	SEM
∞	†	#	Σ	Ж	ξ	●

NA	RLI	MAS	WI	TIV	RDS	UEL
☼	₪	♫	Ξ	§	Θ	Ω

BET		
∞	Ж	■

*	†	Ω

☼	§	╬

Σ	₪	ξ

☺	◉	♫

Ξ	●	#

@	♣	Θ

Answer on page 48

Answers

Page 2

Page 6

For God so loved the world he gave his one and only son that whoever believes in him will never die but have eternal life.

Page 4

Day 1	day night
Day 2	sky
Day 3	land seas plants
Day 4	sun moon stars
Day 5	fish birds
Day 6	animals people

Page 7

Page 5

1. Serpent
2. Fruit
3. Garden
4. Good
5. Evil
6. Ate
7. Trees
8. Where

Hidden message: Sin & Death

Page 8

For to us a child is born, to us a son is given.

Answers

Page 10

He will be great and will be
called the Son of the Most High.

Page 13

Page 11

Page 12

The rising sun will come to us
from heaven to shine on those
living in darkness.

Page 14

God With Us

Page 15

You are to give him the name
Jesus because he will save his
people from their sins.

44

Answers

Page 16

train, boat, feet, car, bus, airplane, bike

Page 18

Mare-Foal, Cow-Calf, Bear-Cub, Swan-Cygnet, Kangaroo-Joey, Sheep-Lamb, Cat-Kitten, Fish-Fingerling, Goose-Gosling, Dog-Puppy, Hen-Chick

Page 19

Today in the town of David a Savior has been born to you.

Page 20

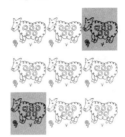

Page 21

Glory to God in the highest, on earth peace to men on whom his favor rests.
Luke 2: 14.

Page 22

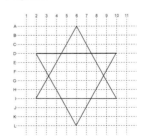

Answers

Page 23

working, baking, faking, looking, joking, cooking, biking, talking, blinking, walking

Page 28

Page 26

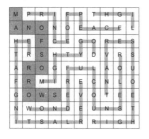

Page 30

Page 27

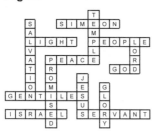

Page 31

Look! The Lamb of God, who takes away the sins of the world.

Answers

Page 32

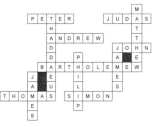

Page 33

Frog, moat, dive, push, joy

Jesus prayed Father forgive them.

Page 34

flashlight, light bulb, rainbow, sunshine, candle, lantern, lightning, campfire, firefly, starlight, sunrise

Page 36

This is how God showed his love among us: He sent his one and only Son into the world.

Page 37

How great is the love of the father that we should be called children of God.

Page 38

Do not be afraid. He is not here. He has risen. (Matthew 28: 7)

Answers

Page 39

Go and make Disciples

Page 40

If you confess with your mouth
"Jesus is Lord" and believe in
your heart that God raised him
from the dead, you will be saved.
Romans 10:9.

Page 42

Bethlehem, Nativity, Christmas,
Shepherds, Immanuel, Starlight,
Wise men